Vampire Kiss

Paul Blum

RISING ★ STARS

'The truth is inside us.
It is the only place where it can hide.'

nasen

NASEN House, 4/5 Amber Business Village, Amber Close,
Amington, Tamworth, Staffordshire B77 4RP

Rising Stars UK Ltd.
22 Grafton Street, London W1S 4EX
www.risingstars-uk.com

Published 2007

Cover design: Button plc
Illustrator: Aleksandar Sotiroski
Text design and typesetting: pentacor**big**
Publisher: Gill Budgell
Editor: Maoliosa Kelly
Editorial consultants: Lorraine Petersen and Cliff Moon

British Library Cataloguing in Publication Data.
A CIP record for this book is available from the British Library.

ISBN: 978-1-84680-256-0

Printed by Craft Print International Limited, Singapore

CHAPTER ONE

Transylvania

The two backpackers stood by the side of a lonely road that led through a creepy forest. It was a dark and wet evening and the only sound they could hear was the howling of wolves. They were lost.

"We're in the middle of nowhere," said Sarah.

"We must find a place to camp before it gets too late," replied Jane.

A few minutes later, a big black car pulled up beside them. The electric window rolled down. The driver spoke to them.

"Good evening," he said. "You're invited to the house of Lord John Snow. I'm his manservant. I'll take you to meet his lordship."

The girls were too tired to ask any questions. They were just happy to get out of the rain on a cold night. Smiling at their good luck, they got into the car.

"Lord Snow must be very rich. This is a great car," said Jane.

At that moment, the car swung around the corner.

"Look at the house!" Sarah exclaimed. "It's like a palace!"

Lord Snow's manservant showed the girls to a very large bedroom.

"Lord Snow is waiting for you in the dining hall," he said.

"This place is incredible!" said Jane. "It's like a pop star's house."

"It's weird how everything is painted black," Sarah added. "It's spooky. It gives me the creeps."

In the dining hall there was a table with three places set on it. Lord Snow stepped out of the shadows and welcomed them.

"Good evening and welcome to my house. I'm happy that you're spending the night as my guests," he said. "What brings you to this place?"

"We're on our gap year," said Jane. "We're taking a walking holiday across Europe."

As they sat down at the table, the two girls could hear the sound of the wind and the wolves howling.

"Why do you live in such a lonely place?" Jane asked.

"I was once a famous rock star," he replied. "I made lots of money and lived a fast life in America. I came here to get away from it all."

"Are you Freddie Cooper?" asked Jane. "My father was a big fan of yours. Weren't you in a band called Vampire?"

"Yes," he said. "But that was a long time ago."

11

Lord Snow poured them a glass of wine each.
The wine tasted good and as they drank it, the girls
began to feel sleepy. Lord Snow walked up and down
in front of the fire. He looked strange in his long, black
cloak and shiny boots.

"When I was young like you, I travelled all over the world," he said. "But now I am old and tired."

"You don't look tired," said Sarah. She was beginning to find Lord Snow a little odd. She noticed his skin was white and his eyes were yellow and bloodshot.

"I feel younger at night," he replied. "When I was a rock star, I slept during the day and came alive at night."

"Well, we've been walking all day, and we need to go to bed now," said Jane. By now she was finding the old man quite frightening.

"In fact, I love the night," Lord Snow continued. "If you listen you can hear the bats flapping outside."

Jane stood up. "Good night and thank you for supper," she said firmly.

"Jane and Sarah, you are so full of life, I envy you." Lord Snow said with tears in his eyes. The girls didn't know what to say as they hurried out of the hall.

The two girls rushed to their room and Jane locked the door.

"You can't be too careful with these old rock stars. They took too many drugs when they were young and they've been a bit crazy ever since," she explained.

"He's just a lonely old man with too much money and time on his hands," Sarah replied. "Tomorrow morning we should ask him to give us a lift in his lovely limo to the nearest youth hostel. I am sure he would do anything we asked him to."

"I'm so sleepy. That wine was really strong," Jane yawned. "Maybe he drugged us."

"Don't be daft! Goodnight, silly. Isn't this bed great?" Sarah replied.

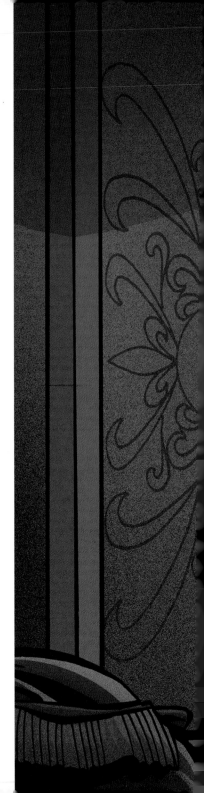

The girls fell into
a deep sleep. The
wind grew stronger
and the wolves
howled louder.
First, the window
blew open and then
the door. A strange
dark shadow entered
the room and bent
down over the girls.
It touched its lips first
to Jane's neck and
then to Sarah's. Then
it bared its teeth
and bit down, sucking
blood from them. Just
before dawn, when it
was no longer thirsty,
it crept silently from
their room.

CHAPTER TWO

A skateboard park in London

Agent Robert Parker and Agent Laura Turnbull worked for MI5, the British Secret Service. On their day off Parker was teaching his partner how to skateboard.

"I'm amazed at just how good you are at this," said Agent Parker. "You've only been doing it for three hours and you're an expert."

"You know me," said Agent Turnbull. "Black belt at karate, junior netball champion at school. I like sports."

"I only wish you were as interested in computers and breaking secret codes," he replied.

"Oh, don't start on about your microchips and giga-bytes," she said. "You must have spent too much of your childhood on a Playstation. Let's go and find ourselves a hot chocolate."

Just as they sat down, Parker's mobile went off.

"We've got to get back to London HQ," he said.
"Commander Watson wants to see us."

"But it's our day off," Turnbull moaned. "And you can't rush a hot chocolate!"

"Two girls have been murdered," Parker explained. "The murderer drained them of their blood."

Turnbull spat out her drink.

"Honestly, Parker, you've got a great sense of timing! You didn't need to tell me that!"

The agents went to see their boss, Commander Watson.

"This looks like a vampire case," said the commander. "The murder victims were on a walking holiday in Transylvania when they were murdered. Their attacker drank all their blood. This isn't the first time something like this has happened. Last year, three girls were murdered in the same way."

"So what do we have to do, Sir?" Turnbull asked Commander Watson.

"You'll go to the scene of the crime. It's a house belonging to Lord John Snow, whose real name is Freddie Cooper. He's a millionaire who made his money as a rock star in the 1970s. You're both too young to remember 'shock horror rock'," Commander Watson explained.

"What's 'shock horror rock'?" asked Turnbull.

"Freddie Cooper had a band called Vampire. They dressed in black and had a weird stage act. Freddie would bite the heads off chickens and pretend to kill young women. It was nasty stuff!" explained their commander, blushing. "But teenagers like me were really into their music!"

"It's good to know you were young once, Sir," joked Turnbull.

"So you want us to check out this Lord John Snow?
Do you think he may be a vampire?" asked Parker.

"I want you to pretend to be backpackers lost in
the woods and find out what's going on,"
Commander Watson explained.

"I guess as I'm a young woman, I'm the perfect bait for
his lordship," Turnbull said.

"You'll have Parker to protect you, as well as full
back-up from London. There's nothing to worry
about," said the commander.

CHAPTER THREE

Transylvania — deep in the forest

"These walking boots are killing me," said Turnbull.

Parker glanced at his watch. "The digital sat-nav shows we're a mile away from Lord Snow's house," he said. "It also shows that there's a graveyard not far from here. Let's take a look."

They shone their torches onto each of the gravestones.

"That's odd," said Parker. "The name on this gravestone is John Snow. Let's take a look inside. If John Snow is a vampire, he'll be up and about by now, as it's night-time."

They pulled off the lid of the tomb. Inside was the body of a man who'd been dead for months.

"What a terrible smell!" Turnbull said, holding her nose.

"Well, *he's* definitely not a vampire!" said Parker.

Parker aimed his camera into the darkness and took some x-ray photos of the body.

"We'll check these out later with London," he said grimly.

The agents left the graveyard and continued along the road to Lord Snow's house.

A long black car pulled up beside them.

"Stretch limo," whispered Turnbull. "Seen more often in New York than in the mountains of Transylvania."

"These vampires have expensive tastes!" Parker joked.

The window of the car rolled down and the agents saw the driver.

"Good evening," said the driver. "You're invited to the house of Lord John Snow. I'm his manservant and I'll take you to meet his lordship."

"Sounds good," said Turnbull and the two agents got into the car.

The manservant showed them to a large bedroom.

"Lord Snow will meet you when you have rested and dressed for dinner," he said.

When he had gone, Agent Turnbull smiled and said, "When I saw we had a double bed I was going to ask for my own room."

"I'll sleep on the floor," said Parker, blushing.

"Don't worry, Parker. After all, we're staying with a vampire and he might as well get two for the price of one!" she said, with a twinkle in her eye.

The agents ate with Lord Snow. They let the old man fill their glasses with wine more than once.

When he wasn't looking, Turnbull poured her wine into a plant and Parker poured his wine into his shoe.

Lord Snow walked up and down in front of the fire. He started talking about his life as a rock star and how old and tired he was feeling now.

"Why Laura, you have a lovely smile. Seeing a young woman like you makes me want to live a little longer," he said with tears in his eyes.

Turnbull yawned loudly.

"You know how to flatter the girls, your lordship," she teased him. "I bet that worked a treat with the groupies when you were a rock star. But if it's all right with you, we must get some sleep now."

When they got to the bedroom, Parker sent
the photographs of the body in the grave to London
in an email from his laptop.

"I've had a reply from London and it's just as
I thought," he said. "The man in the grave *is* John
Snow, alias the rock star Freddie Cooper. The head
wounds show that he was murdered earlier this year."

"So who exactly is our host?" asked Turnbull.

"I think we're about to find out," said Parker grimly.
He turned off the light and took out his gun.

They lay down and pretended to sleep. They waited for a long time in the dark. Outside the wind blew strongly and the wolves howled in the forest.

Suddenly, the door blew open and a dark shadow entered the room and stood by the bed. Behind it, a second shape crawled across the floor.

Parker switched on the light. Lord Snow was holding a pillow over Turnbull's face. The next minute, Turnbull had him in an armlock and was swinging him around.

"We're Secret Service agents! You're under arrest!" she shouted.

A moment later, she knew that she had to let Lord Snow go. Parker was fighting for his life. The manservant had Parker by the throat and was trying to bite him in the neck. Turnbull spun round and karate chopped him until he finally let go. As he ran out of the room, the vampire punched out the light.

The agents switched on their torches. The vampire had gone, leaving Lord Snow lying on the ground, gasping for air.

"You tried to kill me," said Turnbull. "Did you also kill the five girls who were murdered near here?"

"I've nothing to say," he said.

"Are you a vampire?" Parker demanded.

"I'm not a vampire," he replied. "The only vampire around here is Count Otto, my manservant. He's lived in this house for hundreds of years."

"Are you John Snow, otherwise known as Freddie Cooper, the famous rock star?" Turnbull asked and she gave him a very long stare.

"Yes, I am!" he shouted.

"Then listen to this," she

said and she started to sing. When she had finished singing, she asked him another question. "Your band, Vampire, had a number one hit with that song. What's it called?"

"How should I know? It was many years ago. I'm an old man now," John Snow replied.

"You're no more a rock star than I am!" she said. "I'm arresting you for the murder of the real Freddie Cooper alias Lord Snow. Let's go."

41

CHAPTER FOUR

MI5 Headquarters — two weeks later

Agents Parker and Turnbull were working in their office in MI5. Parker was still unhappy about what had happened in Transylvania.

"We still don't know all the answers to the vampire case," Parker said.

"Well, we caught the crook who killed the real Lord Snow and took over his identity," Turnbull replied. "Watson told us that the crook was hoping all the vampire murders would bring tourists back to the area. He wanted to turn the house into a tourist attraction, a new Count Dracula's castle."

"But we still don't know where Count Otto, the vampire manservant went," Parker said.

"He escaped into the woods. Commander Watson put out a swat team but they found nothing," Turnbull reminded him.

"Laura, I found Count Otto's grave in the graveyard the next day, but it was empty! If Otto were a vampire he'd have returned to his grave at dawn. So why wasn't he there? What happened to him?" Parker asked.

The two agents stared at each other. They knew where the conversation was going.

"Don't you see, Laura? This might be a case for The Extraordinary Files," said Parker.

Turnbull nodded. She knew more than she was willing to tell Parker. She didn't tell him that she had seen the swat team take off in a helicopter. She didn't tell him that they had a prisoner on a stretcher with them. She didn't tell him that the prisoner was covered with a sheet and that there was a wooden stake sticking out of his body. Turnbull knew that stabbing a vampire in the heart was the only way to kill it. She didn't tell Parker any of this because she didn't want Parker to get even more angry with MI5 than he already was. Turnbull had known for a long time that things went on in the Secret Service that ordinary agents like them were just not told.

"Something's not right, Laura. I want to get to the bottom of this case," he said.

"You will one day, Robert," she replied. "But how about getting some skateboard practice in first? I'll even let you buy me a hot chocolate."

GLOSSARY OF TERMS

alias an assumed name

crook criminal

Dracula a famous vampire story written by Bram Stoker and set in Transylvania

fast life an indulgent lifestyle

gap year a year off which students take between school and university

groupies fans of a rock group who go to all their concerts

host person who invites someone to stay in their house

HQ headquarters

limo short word for limousine, a long sleek car

MI5 government department responsible for national security

sat-nav satellite-navigator

Secret Service Government Intelligence Department

stake a piece of wood

Transylvania a mountainous region in Romania

vampire a dead body which comes to life at night and drinks the blood of the living

QUIZ

1 Where did Lord John Snow live?

2 What was Lord John Snow's name when he was a rock star?

3 What was the name of Freddie Cooper's rock group?

4 Who was Count Otto?

5 Name three facts you have learnt about vampires

6 Whose body was in the grave?

7 What happened to the real Lord Snow?

8 What was the crook's plan?

9 What happened to Count Otto?

10 How do you kill a vampire?

ABOUT THE AUTHOR

Paul Blum has taught for over 20 years in London inner-city schools.

I wrote The Extraordinary Files for my pupils so they've been tested by some fierce critics (you!). That's why I know you'll enjoy reading them.

I've made the stories edgy in terms of character and content and I've written them using the kind of fast-paced dialogue you'll recognise from television soaps. I hope you'll find The Extraordinary Files an interesting and easy-to-read collection of stories.

ANSWERS TO QUIZ

1 Transylvania

2 Freddie Cooper

3 Vampire

4 Lord Snow's manservant

5 They drink their victim's blood; they only come out at night; they live for hundreds of years

6 The real Lord Snow

7 The crook killed him and took on his identity

8 The crook's plan was to turn the house into a Vampire tourist attraction

9 The Secret Service killed him and took him away

10 Put a wooden stake through the vampire's heart